MW00901344

A NEAL PORTER BOOK

Copyright © 2002 by Yvonne Jagtenberg

Published by Roaring Brook Press
A division of The Millbrook Press, 2 Old New Milford
Road, Brookfield, Connecticut 06804.
First published in the Netherlands by Uitgeverij Hillen,
Amsterdam, as *Mijn konijn*.

All rights reserved

Library of Congress Cataloging-in-Publication Data
Jagtenberg, Yvonne.
Jack's rabbit / Yvonne Jagtenberg.
    p. cm.
A Neal Porter book.
Summary: While Jack is trying to draw a picture of his
pet rabbit, the rabbit runs away, and Jack spends all day
trying to find it.
[1. Rabbits—Fiction. 2. Artists—Fiction.]   I. Title.
PZ7.J153534 Jae 2003
[E]—dc21   2002011958

ISBN 0-7613-1844-5 (trade)
10 9 8 7 6 5 4 3 2 1

ISBN 0-7613-2916-1 (library binding)
10 9 8 7 6 5 4 3 2 1

Printed in Thailand
First American edition 2003

Yvonne Jagtenberg

Jack's Rabbit

A Neal Porter Book
ROARING BROOK PRESS
Brookfield, Connecticut

When Jack's not at school he likes to draw.
He has drawn all kind of things,
but he has not drawn his rabbit.

Jack wants his rabbit to sit still
so he can make a really good drawing
with his best crayon on a big sheet of paper.

But his rabbit doesn't want to sit still.
His rabbit runs away.

And Jack doesn't know where to look.

Jack looks in the backyard.
He looks behind trees.

He looks under chairs and benches.
He still can't find his rabbit.

There is nobody in the street
except for a girl and her dog.
The girl hasn't seen Jack's rabbit.

A boy in the street calls,
"Do you want to play soccer, Jack?"
But Jack doesn't have time. He wants to find his rabbit.

There is a pet shop on the street.

"My rabbit has gone," says Jack.

"You may choose a new rabbit if you want," says the pet shop lady.

But Jack doesn't want a new rabbit.
He wants *his* rabbit.
The best rabbit in the world.

Jack looks for him all afternoon.

He sees lots of rabbits in the sand dunes.

Small gray ones. And brown ones with black spots.
But his rabbit is nowhere to be seen.

On the beach a man is painting.
"Have you seen my rabbit?" Jack asks.
"What does your rabbit look like?" asks the man.

"Big with little brown hair," Jack replies.

"I wanted to draw him, but he ran away.

"Rabbits do as they like," the man says . . . just like the sea."

Jack walks to the park. He is tired.
Some children call, "Look, Jack, look!"
But Jack doesn't want to look. He wants to go home.

A boy pulls Jack's arm.

Jack sees a heap of sand.

And two big legs.

"That's my rabbit!" Jack shouts.
The rabbit looks at Jack. Jack looks at the rabbit.
Rabbits do as they like, Jack thinks.

Jack goes home alone.

But the rabbit wants to come too.

They go home together.

The rabbit is tired—

Tired of all the digging.
He lies down on his cushion and falls asleep.
But Jack isn't tired now. He is drawing his rabbit

with his best crayon on a big sheet of paper.
And underneath it he writes in big letters:

My rabbit

my rabbit